For Viv

First published 2005 by Macmillan Children's Books

This edition published 2005 by Macmillan Children's Books
a division of Macmillan Publishers Limited
20 New Wharf Road, London N1 9RR
Basingstoke and Oxford
Associated companies worldwide
www.panmacmillan.com

ISBN 0 333 99372 1

A CIP catalogue record for this book is available from the British Library.

Printed in Belgium by Proost

Me
and my
Mammoth

Joel Stewart

MACMILLAN CHILDREN'S BOOKS

I like to make things.

But the things I make never seem to turn out how I want.

I've tried paper folding,
but my paper swan was
a bit weird.

I've tried cooking, too, but
Dad's birthday cake wasn't
quite what I'd planned.

I've even tried knitting ... maybe
I should have started with something
easier than a pair of gloves.

Every time I try to make one thing, I end up with
something different. It's very disappointing.

So I decided to get a kit. With instructions and everything,
I couldn't **possibly** get it wrong.

But when I had finished . . .

... it was much **larger** than I expected.

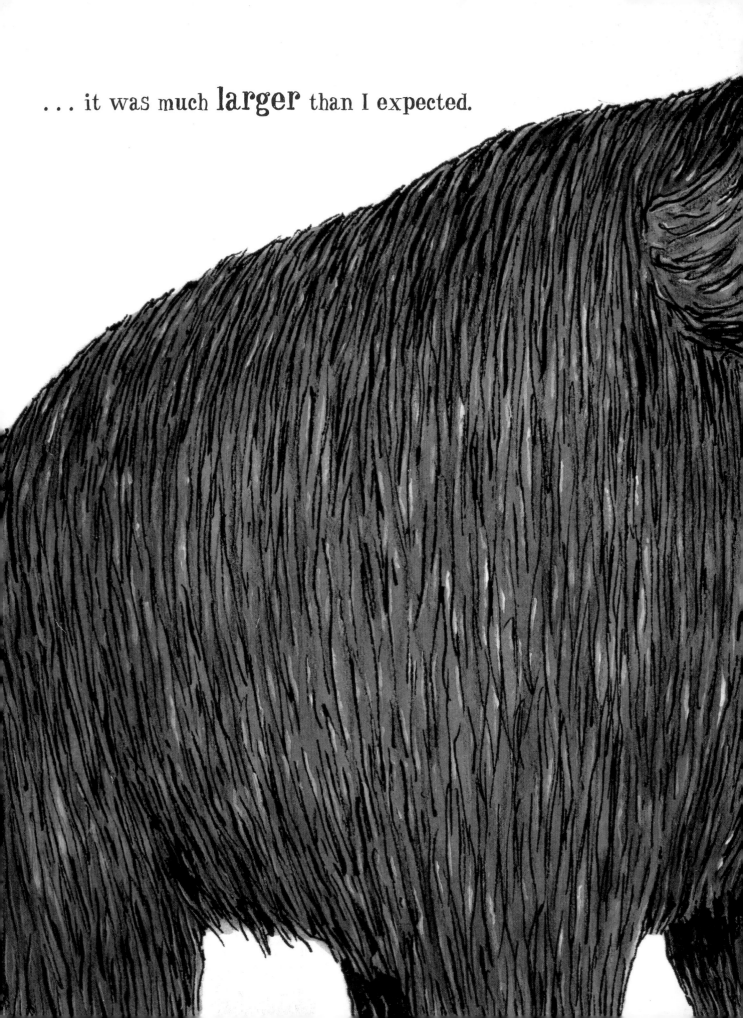

And it was **nothing** like the picture on the box.

I had to put it in the tool shed as there really
isn't room for a mammoth in our house.

The mammoth seemed happy enough.

I think he really liked all the tools – there was an awful lot of banging and hammering going on.

I was too curious to sleep, so I got out of bed . . .

. . . and went to the window.
It seemed that the mammoth
liked making things, too.

And now he wanted me
to come for a ride.

"Don't worry," I thought,
as I struggled aboard.
"Riding a mammoth is just
like riding a hairy bicycle."

Then we left the ground.

I wasn't scared, up above the town on the back of a flying mammoth.

After a while, I even opened my eyes.

What a journey! Flying by mammoth
is THE finest way to travel.

The landing was tricky . . .

But we met some Arctic foxes who were very excited to see us. They gave me some lovely warm clothes.

Then they invited us . . .

...to an **ice sculpture** competition!

Well, I'd never made anything with ice before, and
I like a challenge. I decided to make a graceful ballerina.

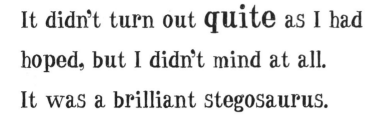

It didn't turn out **quite** as I had
hoped, but I didn't mind at all.
It was a brilliant stegosaurus.

And the Arctic foxes were **VERY** impressed.

Best of all, though . . .

...I made **lots** of new friends!

It was almost time to go home, when the foxes presented
me with their Annual Award for Excellence in Ice Sculpture.
I felt very honoured.

I don't really remember flying
home that night.

But we must have got
back safe and sound.

Since then, I don't really mind if I try to make one thing, and end up with something different.

I still like to make things.

Yes, I like to make them
more than ever.

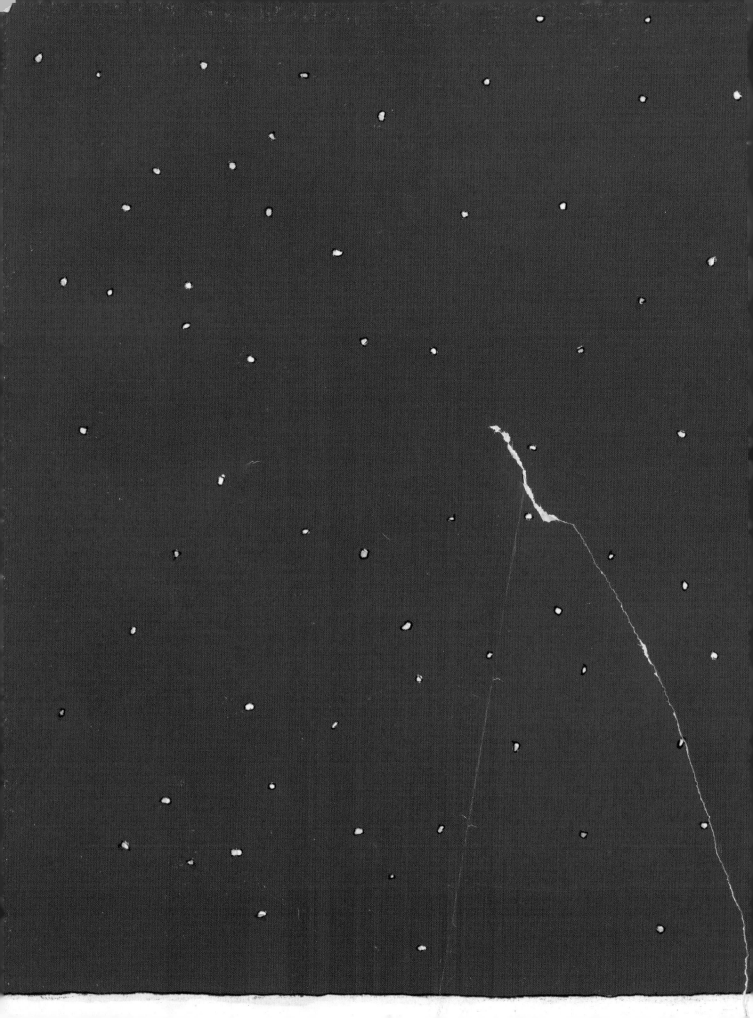